Dear Parents and Educators,

Welcome to Penguin Young Readers! As parents and educators, you know that each child develops at his or her own pace—in terms of speech, critical thinking, and, of course, reading. Penguin Young Readers recognizes this fact. As a result, each Penguin Young Readers book is assigned a traditional easy-to-read level (1–4) as well as a Guided Reading Level (A–P). Both of these systems will help you choose the right book for your child. Please refer to the back of each book for specific leveling information. Penguin Young Readers features esteemed authors and illustrators, stories about favorite characters, fascinating nonfiction, and more!

Bones and the Big Yellow Mystery

LEVEL **3**

GUIDED
READING
LEVEL **K**

This book is perfect for a **Transitional Reader** who:
• can read multisyllable and compound words;
• can read words with prefixes and suffixes;
• is able to identify story elements (beginning, middle, end, plot, setting, characters, problem, solution); and
• can understand different points of view.

Here are some **activities** you can do during and after reading this book:
• Summarize: Using his detective skills, Jeffrey Bones is able to solve the big yellow mystery. Once you've finished reading the book, use your memory to summarize what happened to Mr. Green's bus.
• Character Traits: Bones is the main character in this story. Come up with a list of words to describe him.

Remember, sharing the love of reading with a child is the best gift you can give!

—Bonnie Bader, EdM
  Penguin Young Readers program

*Penguin Young Readers are leveled by independent reviewers applying the standards developed by Irene Fountas and Gay Su Pinnell in *Matching Books to Readers: Using Leveled Books in Guided Reading*, Heinemann, 1999.

For my great-niece, Maayan Malca—DA

For my son, David: Your astounding
talents inspire me—BJN

Penguin Young Readers
Published by the Penguin Group
Penguin Group (USA) Inc., 375 Hudson Street, New York, New York 10014, USA
Penguin Group (Canada), 90 Eglinton Avenue East, Suite 700, Toronto, Ontario M4P 2Y3, Canada
(a division of Pearson Penguin Canada Inc.)
Penguin Books Ltd., 80 Strand, London WC2R 0RL, England
Penguin Group Ireland, 25 St. Stephen's Green, Dublin 2, Ireland (a division of Penguin Books Ltd.)
Penguin Group (Australia), 250 Camberwell Road, Camberwell, Victoria 3124, Australia
(a division of Pearson Australia Group Pty. Ltd.)
Penguin Books India Pvt. Ltd., 11 Community Centre, Panchsheel Park, New Delhi—110 017, India
Penguin Group (NZ), 67 Apollo Drive, Rosedale, Auckland 0632, New Zealand
(a division of Pearson New Zealand Ltd.)
Penguin Books (South Africa) (Pty.) Ltd., 24 Sturdee Avenue,
Rosebank, Johannesburg 2196, South Africa

Penguin Books Ltd., Registered Offices: 80 Strand, London WC2R 0RL, England

Text copyright © 2004 by David A. Adler. Illustrations copyright © 2004 by Barbara Johansen Newman.
All rights reserved. First published in 2004 by Viking and in 2008 by Puffin Books, imprints of
Penguin Group (USA) Inc. Published in 2012 by Penguin Young Readers, an imprint of
Penguin Group (USA) Inc., 345 Hudson Street, New York, New York 10014. Manufactured in China.

The Library of Congress has cataloged the Viking edition
under the following Control Number: 2004000824

ISBN 978-0-14-241042-4   11

PENGUIN YOUNG READERS

LEVEL
TRANSITIONAL
READER
3

BONES

and the Big Yellow Mystery

by David A. Adler

illustrated by Barbara Johansen Newman

Penguin Young Readers
An Imprint of Penguin Group (USA) Inc.

Contents

Chapter 1
My Name Is Bones

My name is Bones.

Jeffrey Bones.

I find clues.

I solve mysteries.

One afternoon I took my detective
bag and went with Grandpa
to the shopping mall.
It's a big place with lots of people
and lots of clues.
We went to the corner store.
I took detective powder
from my detective bag
and sprinkled some on the door.

"Hey, look," I said.

"Fingerprints! Lots of fingerprints!"

"Don't look for clues," Grandpa told me.

"Look for shirts."

"I can do that," I said.

I can read now,

so it's easy for me to find things.

I read the signs.

Signs are clues.

"Follow me," I said,

and Grandpa did.

"Look," I said.

"Lots of shirts!"

"I only need one," Grandpa told me.

I found him the best one.

It had stripes and pockets.

My name is Bones,

Jeffrey Bones.

I find clues.

I find shirts.

"Let's not go home," I said.

"Let's go to the pet shop."

I read the signs and found it.

In the window

was a puppy with curly hair.

"Hello, Curly," I said.

Curly wagged his curly tail.

I took my bad-man disguise

from my detective bag.

I put it on and walked back and forth.

Curly followed me.

I took off my disguise.

"He's a good detective dog," I said.

"He knows how to follow bad men."

"He likes you," Grandpa said.

"I like him, too," I said.

"I want a dog," I told Grandpa,

"but Mom and Dad said I'm too young."

Grandpa nodded.

"Hey, Jeffrey," someone said.

I turned.

It was Mr. Green, my school bus driver.

"Look at Detective Dog Curly," I said.

Mr. Green looked at Curly,

and I looked at Mr. Green.

He looked worried.

Mr. Green said, "I need you."

"Sure you do," I told him.

"Everyone needs Bones."

Chapter 2
I Was Right

Grandpa laughed and said,
"Of course everyone needs bones.
We need bones to stand and walk."

"This is serious," Mr. Green said.

"I lost my bus.

I need Jeffrey to find it."

I took out my pad.

"The big yellow one with wheels?"
I asked.

"Yes," Mr. Green said.

I wrote *Big, Yellow,* and *Wheels*
on my pad.

"A bus is a big thing to lose,"

I told Mr. Green.

"But don't worry.

I find things.

I'll find your bus."

"Maybe someone stole it,"

Mr. Green said.

"Maybe someone did," I told him.

"And maybe not."

I showed him my pad.

"I already have three clues:

Big, Yellow, and *Wheels.*"

I asked Mr. Green to show us
where he left his bus.

"Sure," he said.

"Come with me."

I took out my magnifying glass.

It makes little things big.

It helps me find clues, even little clues.

We followed Mr. Green to the parking lot.

"I left it right there," he said.

He pointed to a row of cars.

"It took up four spots."

I looked through my
magnifying glass.

I didn't see a bus.

But I did see lots of cars.

"These cars are so big," I said.